Faraway Families

By Jena Rhydderch & Jocelyn Tochor

www.farawayfamilies.ca

Faraway Families

Copyright © 2019 by Jena Rhydderch & Jocelyn Tochor

Illustrations by Aveliya Design

All rights reserved. No part of this publication may be reproduced, distributed, or transmitted in any form or by any means, including photocopying, recording, or other electronic or mechanical methods, without the prior written permission of the author, except in the case of brief quotations embodied in critical reviews and certain other non-commercial uses permitted by copyright law.

Tellwell Talent
www.tellwell.ca

ISBN
978-0-2288-1359-0 (Hardcover)
978-0-2288-1322-4 (Paperback)

For our families around the world
~ and to Britton, Maeven, Logan and Baby Gia ~
you are loved, near and far...

Mae and Jae are the best of friends
They live right down the street

They love to play together
Every time they meet

Like so many children
They have family far away

They keep them in their hearts
By sharing memories every day

Jae likes to talk to her cousins
She calls them on the phone

They talk about their days
And how much she has grown

Mae loves to see her grandparents
They video chat from the tub

To share their news and stories
While she learns to wash and scrub

But talking can be tricky
When you live so far away
In some places it is night

In others it is day

It is almost time to visit
Mae counts down the date

Her first trip to a new country
She can hardly wait!

They're off to see their families
Some near, some very far
Mae flies in an airplane

While Jae rides in a car

What fun will they have?
What sights will they see?

They love their family dinners
There is always lots to eat

Lots of hugs and kisses
They love each other so

Time flies by so quickly
Soon it is time to go

It is hard to say goodbye
When you live so far apart

But love stretches as far as you need it
When you look inside your heart

Whether family or friends
Living near or far

You are loved
No matter where you are

My Faraway Family